YOU ARE BEAUTIFUL

Dora Maria Abreu

SKINNY BROWN DOG
MEDIA
EST. 2013
ATLANTA   PUNTA DEL ESTE

First Edition Book, September 2022

ISBN 978-1-957506-42-5 hardback
ISBN 978-1-957506-47-0 paperback

Published by Skinny Brown Dog Media Atlanta, GA
www.skinnybrowndogmedia.com
Distributed by Skinny Brown Dog Media

Dedication

I would like to dedicate this book to my mother who only saw the beauty in all people. And to my family & those who uplift me and others at all times. And lastly to all the beautiful people in this world that they ALL know - they are uniquely beautiful, kind, smart, courageous, strong, brave, resilient, enough and so
loved.

Quisiera dedicar este libro a mi madre que solo veía la belleza en todas las personas. Y a mi familia y aquellos que me animan a mí y a los demás en todo momento. Y, por último, a todas las personas hermosas en este mundo que TODOS sepan que son excepcionalmente hermosas, amables, inteligentes, valientes, fuertes, resistentes, y son profundamente amados.

To Tucker,
Continue to be a light in this world.
EMBRACE Kindness
xoxo
Dora Maria

You are beautiful
Tú eres bello/a

I am beautiful
Yo soy bello/a

You are strong
Tú eres fuerte

I am strong
Yo soy fuerte

You are kind
Tú eres amable

I am kind
Yo soy amable

You are healthy
Tú eres saludable

I am healthy
Yo soy saludable

You are safe
Tú estás a salvo

You are brave

Tú eres valiente

I am brave
Yo soy valiente

You are loved
Tú eres amado/a

I am loved
Yo soy amado/a

You are resilient
Tú eres resistente

I am resilient
Yo soy resistente

You are capable
Tú eres capaz

I am capable
Yo soy capaz

You only compete with yourself
Tú solo compites contigo misma/o

I only compete with myself
Yo solo compito conmigo mismo/a

You have a voice
Tú tienes voz

You can get through anything
Tú puedes superar cualquier cosa

I can get through anything
Yo puedo superar cualquier cosa

You can solve any problem
Tú puedes resolver cualquier problema

I can solve any problem
Yo puedo resolver cualquier problema

You are healthy and strong
Tú eres saludable y fuerte

I am healthy and strong
Yo soy saludable y fuerte

You are enough
Tú eres suficiente

I am enough
Yo soy suficiente

You are thankful
Tú eres agradecida/o

I am thankful
Yo estoy agradecido/a

You are thankful for those around you
Tú estás agradecido/a por todos que te rodean

I am thankful for those around me
Yo estoy agradecido/a por todos que me rodean

You are uniquely you
Tú eres único

I am uniquely Me
Yo soy único

CPSIA information can be obtained
at www.ICGtesting.com
Printed in the USA
JSHW041729220123
36621JS00001B/4